CHILLY STOMACH

CHILLY STOMACH

by Jeannette Caines

pictures by Pat Cummings

Harper & Row, Publishers

Chilly Stomach
Text copyright © 1986 by Jeannette Franklin Caines
Illustrations copyright © 1986 by Pat Cummings
Printed in the U.S.A. All rights reserved.
Designed by Trish Parcell
First Edition
1 2 3 4 5 6 7 8 9 10

Library of Congress Cataloging-in-Publication Data
Caines, Jeannette Franklin.
   Chilly stomach.

   Summary: Whenever Sandy's Uncle Jim comes to visit,
he hugs and kisses her in ways she doesn't like and she
gets a chilly stomach.
   (1. Child molesting—Fiction)   I. Cummings, Pat, ill.
II. Title.
PZ7.C12Ch 1986   (E)   85-45250
ISBN 0-06-020976-3
ISBN 0-06-020977-1 (lib. bdg.)

For Cousin Tillie Harris
and Pat Cummings, of course
J.F.C.

For Robert O. Warren
P.C.

When Uncle Jim tickles me, I don't like it.

Sometimes he hugs me
and kisses me on my lips,
and I get a chilly stomach.

When Daddy and Mommy kiss me
I feel nice and happy and cuddly.

I wish Uncle Jim would never come here.
He's here for dinner every Saturday
And sometimes he stays overnight.

Whenever Uncle Jim stays,
I ask to sleep over at Jill's house.

Jill has an Uncle Fred.
He always hugs and kisses her too.

Jill likes that. They have fun together.

One night I told Jill my secret about Uncle Jim.

At first she said, "Oh, Sandy, he's your uncle!"

But now Jill understands why
I don't feel happy and cuddly with Uncle Jim.

I'm glad I finally told someone.
Jill said she is going to tell her mother,
and that I should tell my parents, too.

I want to tell Mommy and Daddy,
but I'm scared they won't believe me.

I wonder if Jill's mother will tell them.

Maybe Mommy and Daddy
won't like me anymore....

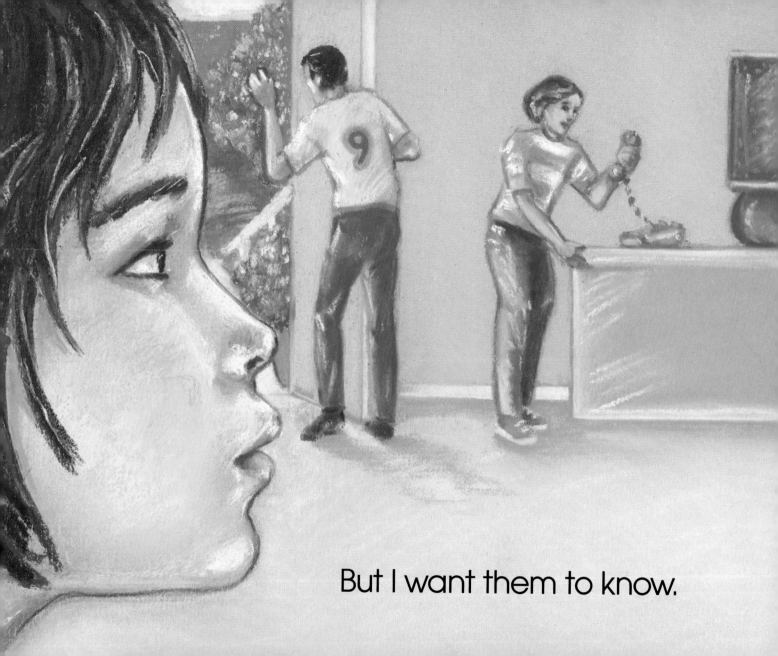

But I want them to know.